This book belongs to

. . . .

For Gabriella

[DK]

A DORLING KINDERSLEY BOOK

First published in Great Britain in 1993
by Dorling Kindersley Limited,
9 Henrietta Street, London WC2E 8PS

Reprinted 1993

Copyright © Susan Winter 1993
The moral right of the author has been asserted

A CIP catalogue record for this book is available from the British Library
ISBN 0-7513-7002-9

Colour reproduction by Dot Gradations
Printed in Belgium by Proost

ME TOO

SUSAN WINTER

DK

DORLING KINDERSLEY
London • New York • Stuttgart

My brother is really clever. . .

He likes reading.

Me too.

He likes building blocks.

Me too.

He likes writing.

Me too.

He likes dressing up.

Me too.

He likes skipping.

Me too.

He likes running.

Me too.

He likes insects.

Me too.

He likes watching scary movies.

Me too.

He likes doing tricks.

Me too.

He needs me.